For Maria and Peter,
Max, Camilla, Anastasia,
and Fen

First U.S. edition 2006

Library of Congress Cataloging-in-Publication Data
is available.

Library of Congress Catalog Card Number pending

ISBN-13: 978-0-7636-3200-7
ISBN-10: 0-7636-3200-7

2 4 6 8 10 9 7 5 3 1

Printed in Singapore

This book was typeset in Stone Print Roman.
The illustrations were done in colored pencil and pastel.

Candlewick Press
2067 Massachusetts Avenue
Cambridge, Massachusetts 02140

visit us at www.candlewick.com

A PUPPY for ANNIE

Kim Lewis

CANDLEWICK PRESS
CAMBRIDGE, MASSACHUSETTS

One day a girl named Annie fell in
love with a puppy named Bess.
"Can I take her home with me?"
asked Annie.

Bess came home to a
small house on a hill.
She sniffed the air and
wagged her tail.
"What is Bess trying
to say?" asked Annie.
"Just watch and you'll
see," said Mom.

Bess followed Annie wherever she went.

When Annie stopped walking, Bess flopped at her feet.

"What does Bess want?" asked Annie.

Mom smiled. "Bess wants to be next to you."

So Annie stroked Bess
and tickled her ears.

Soon Bess went snooping all around the house.
She tugged at the pots and pans. She chewed on
the shoes and rolled in the rug.
Annie laughed. "What does Bess want?"
"Bess wants to play," said Mom.
So Annie found Bess some toys of her own.

When Mom and Annie sat down for their lunch,
Bess found out how to say she was hungry.
She rattled her bowl and looked up at Annie.
"I know what you want," said Annie.
So Annie fed Bess, and
they all ate together.

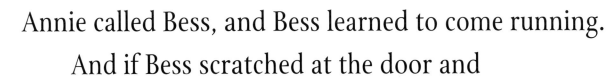

Annie called Bess, and Bess learned to come running.
And if Bess scratched at the door and
sniffed the boots, Annie knew what
Bess wanted most of all in the world.
"Time to go out," she
said to her dog.

Bess leaped a lot, full of nothing but joy.
So did her best friend, Annie.
They ran every day to their wild
special places, where a girl and her
dog could explore for hours.
And the world, right then,
belonged to Bess and Annie.

But one day as they sat down
to rest, Annie told Bess she
would be going to school soon.
Bess would be alone with
Mom during the day.
Annie stroked Bess for
as long as she could.

Then the day came, and
Annie was gone.
Bess scratched at the door.
She sniffed Annie's boots.
She played with her toys,
but it wasn't the same.

Bess went to Mom and lay at her feet.

"Annie won't be long," said Mom.

She gently stroked Bess and tickled her ears.

Bess curled in a ball.

She waited, asleep.

At the sound of the old
school bus, Bess leaped a lot,
full of nothing but joy.
She ran to Annie without
being called. She wagged
her tail hard. She wagged
all over. Mom laughed.
"What does Bess want?"
"Bess wants me!"
said Annie.

So Annie and Bess went walking together.
And the world, right then, all over again,
belonged to just Bess and Annie.